D1095675

THE LIBRARY OF PHYSICAL SCIENCE™

Looking at Atoms and Molecules

Suzanne Slade

The Rosen Publishing Group's
PowerKids Press™
New York

To Meghan and Ryan Slade

Published in 2007 by The Rosen Publishing Group, Inc.
29 East 21st Street, New York, NY 10010

First Edition

Editor: Amelie von Zumbusch
Book Design: Elana Davidian
Layout Design: Ginny Chu
Photo Researcher: Gabriel Caplan

Photo Credits: Cover © Mei Yates/Taxi/Getty Images; p. 4 JPL-NASA; p. 5 © Kenneth Eward/BioGrafx/Photo Researchers, Inc.; p. 6 © Mary Evans Picture Library/The Image Works; pp. 7, 13 © SSPL/The Image Works; p. 8 LADA/Hop Americain/Photo Researchers, Inc.; p. 9 © Custom Medical Stock Photo; p. 10 © CDC/PHIL/Corbis; p. 11 © Steve Gschmeissner/Science Photo Library/Photo Researchers, Inc.; p. 12 DOE Photo; p. 14 © Tek Image/Photo Researchers, Inc.; p. 15 Digital Instruments/Veeco/Photo Researchers, Inc.; p. 16 © John Nordell/The Image Works; p. 17 © Roger Ressmeyer/Corbis; p. 18 © Emely/zefa/Corbis; p. 19 © Graham J. Hills/Science Photo Library/Photo Researchers, Inc.; p. 20 © Kenneth Eward/Photo Researchers, Inc.; p. 21 © Fermilab/Photo Researchers, Inc.

Library of Congress Cataloging-in-Publication Data

Slade, Suzanne.
  Looking at atoms and molecules / Suzanne Slade.— 1st ed.
      p. cm. — (The Library of physical science)
  Includes index.
  ISBN 1-4042-3419-5 (library binding) — ISBN 1-4042-2166-2 (paperback)
  1. Microscopes—Juvenile literature. 2. Atoms—Juvenile literature. 3. Molecules—Juvenile literature. I. Title. II. Series.
  QH211.S73 2007
  502.8'2—dc22
                                                    2005035107

Manufactured in the United States of America

Contents

What Is an Atom?

Everything in the world is made of tiny **particles** called atoms. Atoms are the tiny building blocks that create every solid, liquid, and gas. Your body and the air you breathe are made of atoms. Although atoms make up everything you see, you cannot see an atom. Atoms are so small that millions of them would fit inside the period at the end of this sentence.

There are 94 different kinds of atoms that

All matter, including Earth and the Moon, is made up of tiny atoms.

occur naturally. Atoms combine with other atoms in many ways to make the millions of things you see in the world. When one atom has joined with one or more other atoms, it is called a

A molecule of oxygen gas is made up of two oxygen atoms joined together.

molecule. Some molecules are small. For example, a molecule of **oxygen** gas is made of just two oxygen atoms. Other molecules are very large. A molecule of table sugar is made of three different kinds of atoms and has a total of 45 atoms.

Using Scientific Instruments

Through the years scientists have searched for ways to study tiny objects such as atoms. Scientists invented special scientific instruments called **microscopes** to help them look at very small things. Microscopes magnify things, or make things look larger than they really are.

Zacharias Janssen, shown here, and his father, Hans, lived in Middleburg, Holland. They were eyeglasses makers.

The first major scientific instrument scientists used was the **compound** microscope. Hans and Zacharias Janssen, a father and his son, invented the compound microscope around 1590.

A compound microscope has two or more lenses and shines a light on the object it magnifies. It can magnify an object up to 1,000 times. Scientists use a compound microscope to magnify cells, the tiny parts that make up plants and animals.

However, a compound microscope cannot magnify something as small as an atom or a molecule. Compound microscopes are commonly found in homes and schools. You may have used one to look at pieces of dust or the wings on a bug.

Over time scientists made many improvements to the compound microscope. The compound microscope shown here was made around 1700.

The Electron Microscope

After the invention of the compound microscope, scientists worked hard to make a more powerful scientific instrument. Around 1932, scientists in Germany built a new kind of microscope called an **electron** microscope. It shot a beam of electrons, instead of light, at the object being viewed. The electron beam allowed scientists to see smaller objects.

This first electron microscope did not give a very clear image, or picture, of the object it

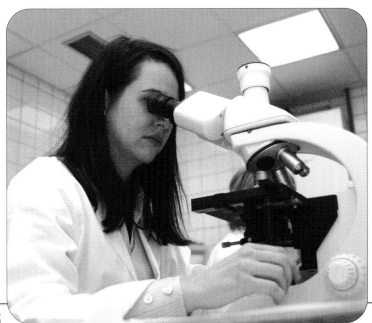

Electron microscopes have many uses. This scientist is using an electron microscope to look at blood cells.

was magnifying. A few years later, scientists made an improved electron microscope, which they called a **transmission** electron microscope (TEM). A TEM is smaller than an electron microscope. An object must be cut into very thin pieces to be magnified with a TEM. That is because an electron beam must be able to pass through the object. A TEM can magnify objects 500,000 times. It shows a flat image of the object. Scientists saw an image of a molecule for the first time with a TEM.

This thin piece of an object has been prepared for a TEM.

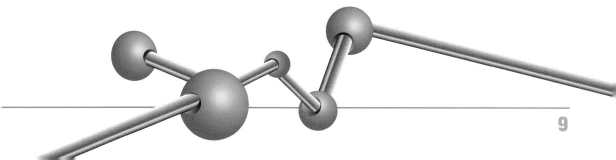

The Scanning Electron Microscope

In the 1960s, scientists improved the TEM. They made a kind of microscope that used an electron beam to make an object send out electrons from its surface. Scientists named this kind of microscope a **scanning** electron microscope (SEM).

An SEM can create a magnified image using an entire object, instead of just a thin piece of

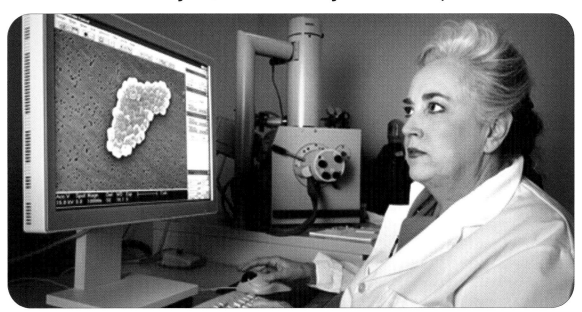

This scientist is using an SEM to study a type of cell that makes people sick.

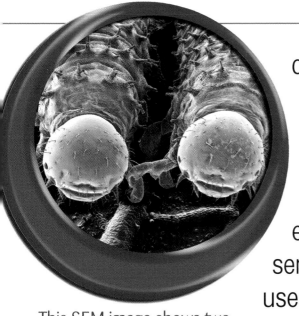

This SEM image shows two caterpillars on a leaf.

an object. An SEM can magnify any part of the object's surface. Instruments in an SEM keep track of the electrons an object sends off. The microscope uses these electrons to create an image on a screen. An SEM cannot magnify objects as many times as a TEM can. The advantage of an SEM is that it gives a three-dimensional image. A three-dimensional image shows how tall, wide, and thick something is. These images are used in many ways. For example, the images of different metals help builders choose the right metal for a certain job.

The Scanning Tunneling Microscope

The scanning tunneling microscope, called the STM, was invented in 1981 by Gerd Binnig and Heinrich Rohrer. An STM can magnify an object 500 million times. It gives scientists an image of individual atoms on the surface of an object.

The needle on an STM moves across the surface of the object being magnified. The tip of this needle is made of tungsten, a very strong metal. The tungsten tip moves over an object. It measures the small

You can see the individual atoms in this STM image. An STM colors the images of atoms so that they are easy to see.

This STM was made in 1986. Scientists often use STMs to study the surface of metals.

amount of electric charge that flows between the tungsten atoms and the object's atoms. Because an STM uses an electric charge, it can only magnify objects that conduct electricity. The STM is the first kind of microscope that can move individual atoms. Scientists have built tiny objects with STMs, such as a guitar the size of a human cell. Someday scientists hope to use the STM to build very small machines.

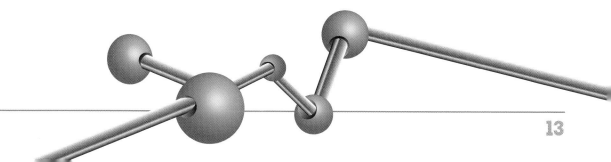

The Atomic Force Microscope

Calvin Quate, Gerd Binnig, and Christoph Gerber invented a new kind of microscope called the atomic force microscope (AFM) in 1986. Much like an STM, an AFM has a needle that moves over the object that is being magnified. The tip of the needle is made of the element silicon or the silicon compound silicon nitrate. An STM can be used only on objects that conduct electricity, but an AFM can be used on any object.

As STMs are, AFMs are often used to study metals. However because AFMs can study matter that does not conduct electricity, they can also be used to study plant and animal cells.

This image of an orange tip butterfly's wing was made by an AFM.

An AFM needs certain conditions to create clear images. This kind of microscope takes very exact measurements. Small movements in the room can cause it to make a mistake. For this reason scientists place AFMs inside rooms that guard them from these tiny movements. An AFM shows images of the atoms on an object's surface on a computer screen. The computer adds color to the image to help scientists see the shape of the atoms on an object's surface.

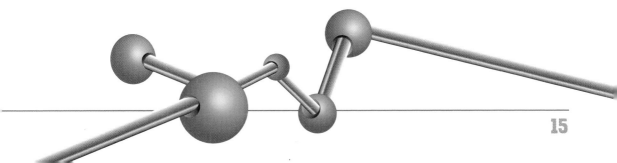

The Confocal Microscope

In the late 1980s scientists built a new kind of microscope called the **confocal** microscope. This microscope came from an idea that Marvin Minsky had in the 1950s. It took more than 30 years of work and the invention of the laser for the confocal microscope to be built. A laser is a strong, focused, or fixed, beam of light.

A confocal microscope gives scientists three-dimensional images of objects. These images are much clearer than images from earlier microscopes. As many microscopes have, a

Marvin Minsky, seen here, studies computers. He is working to create a computer that can think like a person.

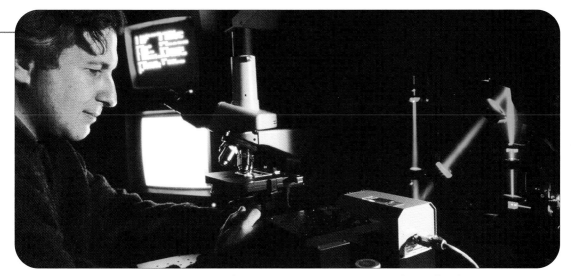

This scientist is using a confocal microscope to study cells that carry messages from the brain throughout the body.

confocal microscope has a lens called an objective lens. This lens focuses the laser or, in an electron microscope, the electrons on the object that is being magnified. A confocal microscope works so well because it can focus the laser on all the different parts of an object's surface. Scientists can look at many objects, including living things, with a confocal microscope. Images from a confocal microscope appear on a computer screen.

Atoms in Well-ordered Arrays

By using microscopes and other scientific instruments, scientists have learned a lot about how atoms join to form objects. One discovery they made is that the atoms in some solids arrange themselves in patterns. Scientists use the term "well-ordered array" to describe how these patterns of atoms are arranged.

A honeycomb, shown here, is an example of a well-ordered array that occurs in nature.

You may have learned about arrays in math. An array is an arrangement of objects in straight rows that are

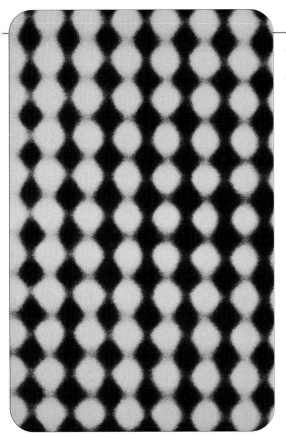

next to each other. For example, a dozen eggs in a box is an array with two straight lines of six eggs. Arrays can have several shapes, such as a square, rectangle, or hexagon. A hexagon is a shape with six equal sides. A box of 24 cans of soda in which the cans roll out of a hole at the bottom holds the cans in a hexagonal array. "Well-ordered" means "neatly arranged." A well-ordered array has many rows of arrays neatly lined up next to each other.

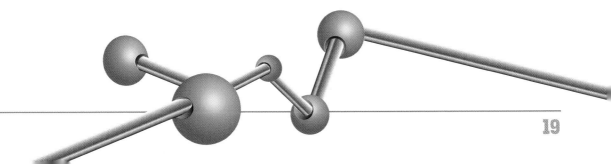

Smashing Atoms

Scientists also use an instrument called a particle **accelerator** to study atoms. A particle accelerator speeds atoms up until they are moving very fast. Then the accelerator causes the atoms to smash into a **target** and break into pieces.

Electrons circle around particles called protons and neutrons in the center of an atom.

As the atoms break apart, scientists can study the particles inside the atoms. These particles include **protons**, **neutrons**, and electrons. Scientists can also learn about the forces that hold these particles together.

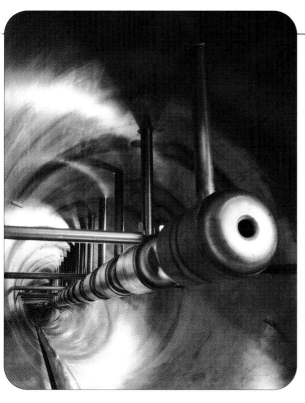

This is a view of the inside of a linear accelerator at the Fermi National Accelerator Laboratory, outside of Chicago.

There are two kinds of particle accelerators, **circular** and **linear**. Circular accelerators were invented first, around 1929. Circular accelerators speed an atom up around a track that is shaped like a circle. When the atom is traveling fast enough, a target is placed in its path. This causes the atom to break into pieces. In a linear accelerator, an atom travels down a long, metal tube before hitting a target and breaking apart. Linear accelerators are very long and are located under the ground.

Scientific Instruments of Tomorrow

Throughout history people have been curious about things that are too small to see. Scientists have been using microscopes since the 1500s. Today there are more than 40 different kinds of microscopes that scientists can use. They continue to invent powerful tools to look at small objects like atoms.

Scientists are now working to create very small microscopes. A tiny microscope called a micro-CIA has a lens about the size of a piece of salt. Scientists hope small microscopes will allow doctors to look inside a sick person's body, so they will be better able to heal that person. Scientists in the coming years will make better scientific instruments. It is exciting to imagine the new discoveries they will make about the things we cannot see.

Glossary

accelerator (ik-SEH-luh-ray-ter) Something that increases the speed of something else.

circular (SER-kyuh-ler) Having the form of a circle.

compound (KOM-pownd) Having to do with two or more things combined.

confocal (kun-FOH-kul) Having to do with two or more things that have the same focus.

electron (ih-LEK-tron) Having to do with a particle inside an atom that spins around the center of an atom.

linear (LIH-nee-er) Like a straight line.

microscopes (MY-kruh-skohps) Instruments used to see very small things.

neutrons (NOO-tronz) Particles with a neutral electric charge found in the center of an atom.

oxygen (OK-sih-jen) A gas that has no color, taste, or odor and is necessary for people and animals to breathe.

particles (PAR-tih-kulz) Small pieces of something.

protons (PROH-tonz) Particles with a positive electric charge found in the center of an atom.

scanning (SKAN-ing) Looking closely at something.

target (TAR-git) Something that is aimed at.

transmission (tranz-MIH-shun) Causing something to be passed through something else.

Index

Web Sites

Due to the changing nature of Internet links, PowerKids Press
has developed an online list of Web sites related to the subject
of this book. This site is updated regularly. Please use this link
to access the list:

www.powerkidslinks.com/lops/instrum/